D0504791

7

8

9

10

11

12

To David with great love and thanks for almost everything

First published in Great Britain in 2003 by Simon & Schuster UK Ltd
Africa House, 64-78 Kingsway, London WC2B 6AH

First published in 2003 by Atheneum Books for Young Readers,
an imprint of Simon & Schuster Children's Publishing Division, New York

A CIP catalogue record for this book is available from the British Library upon request.

Book design by Ann Bobco
The text for this book was set in Centaur.
The illustrations are rendered in charcoal and gouache on paper.

ISBN 0689837372

Manufactured in the United States of America

1 3 5 7 9 10 8 6 4 2

Grateful acknowledgment to:
• The Griffith Institute, Oxford, for permission to use the photo on p. 7 of the Sphinx.
• Barbara Morgan Archives for permission to use the photo on p. 9 of Martha Graham, *Letter to the World*
(Kick), 1940, copyright © Barbara Morgan, Barbara Morgan Archives.

. . . and the Missing Toy

by Ian Falconer

Simon & Schuster

London New York Sydney

One day Olivia was riding a camel in Egypt . . .

when her mother woke her up.
"Time to get up, sweetie-pie.
Remember, you have football
this morning."

Olivia's uniform comes in a really unattractive green.

"Mummy, can you make
me a red football shirt
like this one? Please? . . ."

"But then you'll look
different from everyone
else on the team,"
explained her mother.

"That's the point."

When Olivia came home
from practice, her mother
was working on the shirt.
"Is it done yet?" she asked.
"Not yet," said her mother.

Olivia waited,

and waited,

and waited,

till she was too exhausted to wait any longer.

So she went out to play with the cat.

"Look, darling, it's all done!" said her mother.

But something was missing.
"Wait a second," said Olivia.

“Where’s my toy?”

"Where's my toy? It was right there on the bed. I just put it there. I remember exactly. That's my best toy. I need it now! Somebody took my best toy!"

Olivia looked everywhere –

under the rug,

under the sofa,

under the cat.

She asked her little brother, Ian,
"WHAT DID YOU DO WITH MY TOY?"

She asked her baby brother, William,

"WHAT DID YOU DO WITH MY TOY?"

"Wooshee gaga."

That night,
and it was a dark and stormy night,
Olivia was practising her piano
when she heard an awful sound.

The sound got louder
and louder.
It was
HORRIBLE,
and it was coming
from behind
the door.

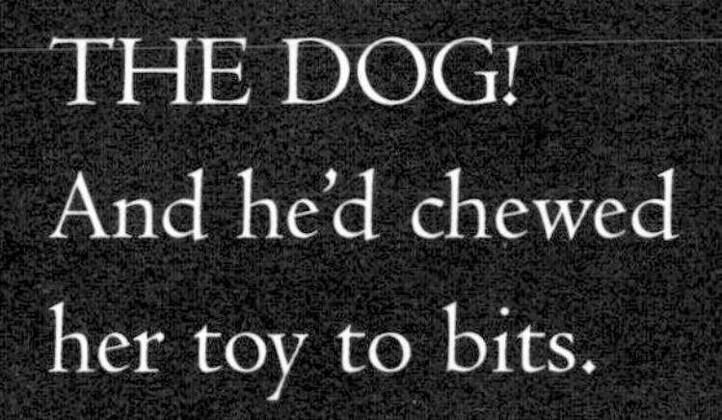

THE DOG!
And he'd chewed
her toy to bits.

And that's when
she saw it. It was . . .

So, of course, Olivia went inside.

"Mummy, Daddy, Mummy, Daddy! It was Perry!" cried Olivia.
"He took my best toy and chewed it to bits, and now it's broken."

"I'm sorry, sweetie-pie," said her mother, "but doggies like to chew.
And he didn't know it was your toy."

"My *best* toy."

"Don't worry," said Olivia's father.
"Tomorrow we'll go get you the *very* best toy in the whole world."

"Oh, thank you, Daddy. I love you more than anyone."

Still, it *was* Olivia's best toy. So she fixed it,

adding a bow for extra beauty.

All better.

"Only books about cats tonight, Mummy."

But even Olivia couldn't stay angry forever.

1

2

3

4

5

6